READ TO TIGER

by S. J. Fore

illustrated by R. W. Alley

VIKING

An Imprint of Penguin Group (USA) Inc.

E FOR

CLICK!

For M and P . . . and for TM, who always adds a smile to my day.
— S.J.F.

To my uncle Bob, who was always comfortable expounding from a sofa.
— R.W.A.

Viking

Published by Penguin Group
Penguin Young Readers Group, 345 Hudson Street, New York, New York 10014, U.S.A.
Penguin Group (Canada), 90 Eglinton Avenue East, Suite 700, Toronto, Ontario, Canada M4P 2Y3 (a division of Pearson Penguin Canada Inc.)
Penguin Books Ltd, 80 Strand, London WC2R 0RL, England
Penguin Ireland, 25 St Stephen's Green, Dublin 2, Ireland (a division of Penguin Books Ltd)
Penguin Group (Australia), 250 Camberwell Road, Camberwell, Victoria 3124, Australia (a division of Pearson Australia Group Pty Ltd)
Penguin Books India Pvt Ltd, 11 Community Centre, Panchsheel Park, New Delhi - 110 017, India
Penguin Group (NZ), 67 Apollo Drive, Rosedale, North Shore 0745, Auckland, New Zealand (a division of Pearson New Zealand Ltd.)
Penguin Books (South Africa) (Pty) Ltd, 24 Sturdee Avenue, Rosebank, Johannesburg 2196, South Africa

Penguin Books Ltd, Registered Offices: 80 Strand, London WC2R 0RL, England

First published in 2010 by Viking, a division of Penguin Young Readers Group

1 3 5 7 9 10 8 6 4 2

Text copyright © S. J. Fore, 2010
Illustrations copyright © R. W. Alley, 2010
All rights reserved

LIBRARY OF CONGRESS CATALOGING-IN-PUBLICATION DATA
Fore, S. J.
Read to tiger / by S. J. Fore ; illustrated by R. W. Alley.
p. cm.
Summary: A little boy who wants to read his book keeps being distracted by a tiger
who is busy chomping on gum, growling, and practicing karate kicks.
ISBN 978-0-670-01140-7 (hardcover)
[1. Books and reading—Fiction. 2. Tigers—Fiction.] I. Alley, R. W. (Robert W.), ill. II. Title.
PZ7.F75812Re 2010
[E]—dc22
2009035147

Manufactured in China
Set in Typeka
Book design by Nancy Brennan

I sit down on the couch
and open my book.
It's time to read . . .

But I **can't** read,
because there's a tiger
behind my couch ...

"Huh-uh, Tiger." I shake my head.
"Please spit out your gum.
I want to read my book.
And I can't think
when you chomp."

"Oops," the tiger says.
"Tiger is sorry.
Tiger won't chomp!"

The chomping stops.
I try to read my book . . .

But I **can't** read my book,
because I hear...

I can't read my book,
because there's a tiger behind my couch
pretending to be a bear.

"Huh-uh, Tiger! Please take off
my bear costume right now!
You're going to rip it!

And will you please
stop growling!"
I tell the tiger.
"I can't concentrate.
Can't you see that I'm trying to read?"

"Ooops!" the tiger says.

"Tiger is sorry.
Tiger won't be a bear anymore!"

The tiger takes off my bear costume
and stops growling.
I pick up my book again and try to read.

But it's very hard to read when there's a Karate Tiger

HI-YA!

behind your couch...

HI-YA!

"TIGER! STOP!

Now isn't a good time to work
on your karate kicks!
I want to read my book!"

"Ooops!

Tiger is very sorry!
Tiger won't do karate kicks.
No more Karate Tiger!"

The tiger stops hi-yaaa-ing.
I try to read.
But coming around my couch . . .

Choo-Choo
choo-Choo
choo-
Choo

"Huh-uh! Tiger!
Get off that train right now!
Stop choo-chooing and
stop toot-tooting!
I want to read!
Can't you be quiet?"

"**Oooooooops!**

Tiger is very sorry!
Tiger can be quiet!" the tiger says.

The tiger stops choo-chooing
and toot-tooting.

I try to read my book again.
Suddenly . . .

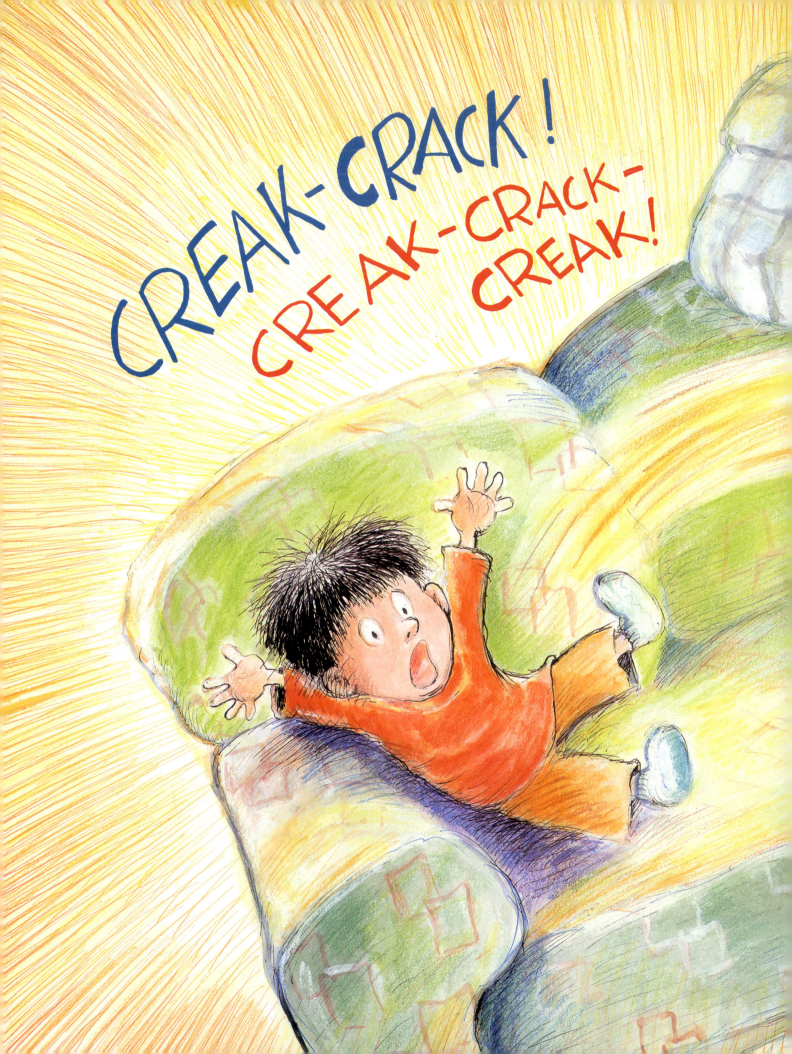

My couch is flying up in the
air, because there's a tiger
under it.

"TIGER!
Put me down!

What in the world are you doing
under the couch?"

"Tiger is looking for the whistle!
Tiger lost it!"
the tiger sniffles.

I help the tiger
find the whistle.

Then I say, "Tiger,
PLEASE sit down right here!
And be very, VERY quiet,
so I can read my book!
OKAY?"

"Okay . . . Tiger will sit down!
Tiger will be VERY, very, very quiet,"
the tiger whispers.

The tiger plops down on the floor in front of me.

And he is

VERY

very

quiet.

He doesn't make another sound.

No **chomp-chomp-chomping.**

No **grrrr-grrr-grrr-ing**

No **hi-ya! hiii-yaaaaa-ing.**

No **choo-choo-choo-TOOTING.**

Not even any

CREAK-CRACK CREAK-CRACKING . . .

I hold my book up
in front of my face,
so I can't see the tiger.
I try to concentrate.

All of a sudden, I think
I see a little shadow on my
book . . .

I do see a shadow.

Then I think I see
a whisker . . .

I do see a whisker.

Then I see a nose . . .
Then I see a whole tiger
in front of my book.

"Tiiiiiiger!

What are you doing?
You're in the way!

I can't see my book!

I AM TRYING TO READ!"

"What's that?" the tiger asks.
The tiger points to a picture in my book.

"That's the tiger in the story," I tell him.

"A TIGER!?"

the tiger shouts.

Then he

JUMPS

onto the couch.

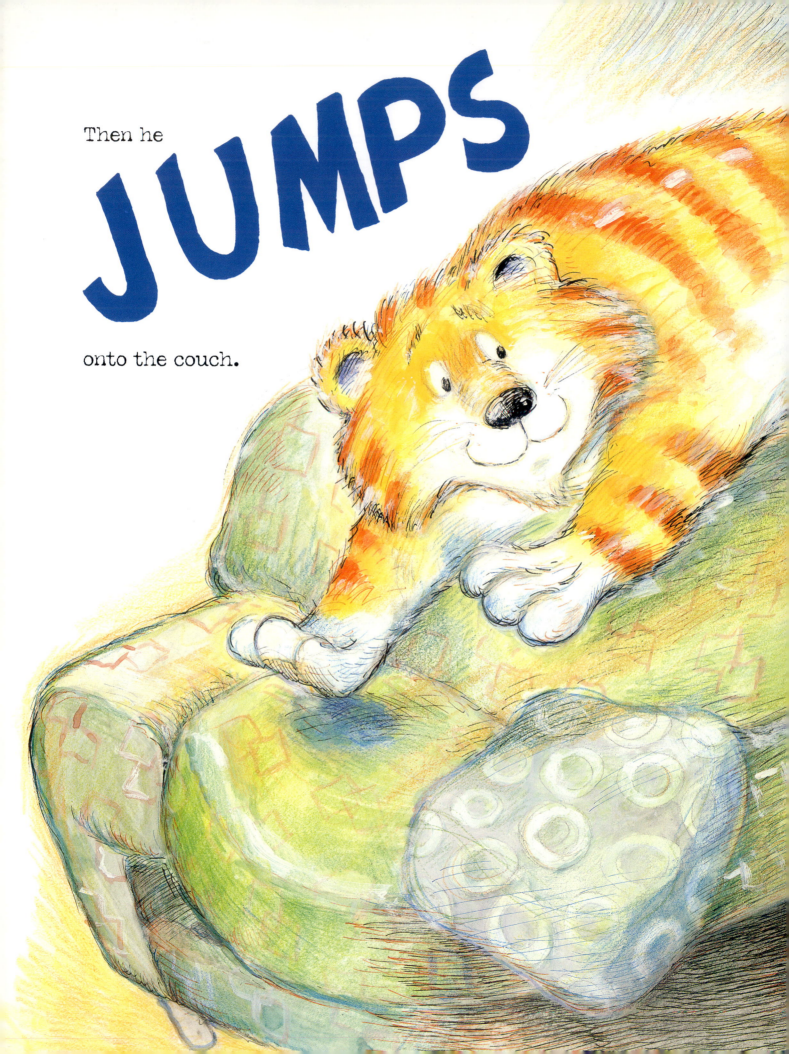

He fluffs the couch cushions
and curls up beside me.

And finally I can read my book . . .
to Tiger.